ILLUMINATION PRESENTS

DESPICABLE ME3™

Seek and Find

Written by Trey King
Art by Fractured Pixels
Based on the Motion Picture Screenplay by
Cinco Paul and Ken Duario

LITTLE, BROWN & COMPANY
LB kids

Little, Brown and Company
Hachette Book Group
1290 Avenue of the Americas, New York, NY 10104
Visit us at lb-kids.com
www.despicable.me

First Edition: May 2017

LB kids is an imprint of Little, Brown and Company.
The LB kids name and logo are trademarks of Hachette Book Group, Inc.

The publisher is not responsible for websites (or their content) that are not owned by the publisher.

ISBN: 978-0-316-50768-4 (paper over board)

Printed in the United States of America

PHX

10 9 8 7 6 5 4 3 2 1

The Minions are back!

**So are Gru, Lucy, and the girls. They are ready for mayhem.
Are you?**

**Throughout this book, you'll need to help seek and find everything
from hidden treasure to pink pigs to stuffed unicorns. But the
most important thing to find is bananas. Minions love bananas,
and you'll find 10 bananas hidden on every page.**

Good luck!

FUN IN THE SUN!

Grucy (that means Gru *and* Lucy) just foiled Balthazar Bratt's plan to steal the world's largest diamond. Minions Jerry and Dave tried to help, but they got distracted—and started a dance party on the beach!

CAN YOU SPOT:

BAD DAY AT THE OFFICE

The AVL has a new boss in charge, and her name is Valerie Da Vinci! She does not like Gru, and decides to fire him. Lucy tries to help, and is fired, too.

CAN YOU SPOT:

SURPRISE HONEYMOON

When Gru and Lucy get home, the girls have a surprise planned for them. Since they never had a honeymoon, the girls made a tiki party in the backyard. They even made gummy-bear-and-meat soup. Yum?

CAN YOU SPOT:

MINIONS ON STRIKE!

Gru tells the Minions he lost his job. Mel and the other Minions are excited for their master to return to his evil ways—except Gru doesn't plan on doing that. Now Mel is organizing a strike!

CAN YOU SPOT:

THE BEST BEDROOM EVER

Every night, Gru tucks the girls into bed and reads Agnes a bedtime story. Their room is filled with fun things. Don't you wish your room were this awesome?!

CAN YOU SPOT:

12

WELCOME TO FREEDONIA!

Gru, Lucy, and the girls (and Jerry and Dave) go to Freedonia to meet Gru's long-lost twin brother, Dru! It turns out the family business is (can you guess?) pig farming!

CAN YOU SPOT:

FREEDONIA CHEESE FESTIVAL

Gru and Dru want to spend some together time on their own. So Lucy takes the girls out for a day of fun...at the local cheese festival! They have singing and dancing and...cheese jewelry? (Do you wear it or eat it?)

CAN YOU SPOT:

GET THAT PIZZA!

The Minions are *sooooooo* hungry. But they don't have jobs, and they don't have money, and their tiny, yellow tummies keep growling. What's that smell? A pizza delivery boy! Get him!

CAN YOU SPOT:

SING A SONG, MINIONS!

In the middle of the chase, the Minions end up on the stage of a popular talent show. Do they have what it takes to impress the judges and the fans? Or will the cops get them first?

CAN YOU SPOT:

SECURITY

BAD-BOY BLUES

Some of the Minions went to jail. But it's not fun at all, so they have to try to make their own fun. They soon realize they miss Gru and the outside world. Looks like being bad wasn't worth it! Crime doesn't pay.

CAN YOU SPOT:

The End? Nope!

We have a few more things hidden for you. Go back for another look and see if you can spot these extra-fun things.

CAN YOU SPOT:
an oyster with a pearl

CAN YOU SPOT:
parachuting pizza

CAN YOU SPOT:
6 pineapples

CAN YOU SPOT:
5 paper airplanes

CAN YOU SPOT:
a butterfly painting

CAN YOU SPOT:
propeller hat

CAN YOU SPOT:
boy wearing pig nose

CAN YOU SPOT:
fire hydrant

CAN YOU SPOT:
juggling Minion

CAN YOU SPOT:
cupcake